FRAIDY-CAT

"Lois," Jessica said, as Elizabeth, Lila, and Lois caught up to her. She was standing in front of the Brants' driveway. "See that apple tree over there?" she said.

Lois nodded.

"If you climb it and get some apples for all of us, you can—"

"No way!" Elizabeth interrupted. "You know we aren't supposed to climb trees in other peoples' yards."

Jessica shrugged her shoulders. "It doesn't matter. Lois wouldn't do it anyway."

"That's right," Lila added. "Lois is too much of a fraidy-cat to do an easy thing like that."

Lois pulled on her sweater nervously. "I'll do it," she whispered. She gulped and reached for a branch.

Bantam Skylark Books in the
SWEET VALLEY KIDS series
Ask your bookseller for the
books you have missed

SWEET VALLEY KIDS

CRYBABY LOIS

Written by
Molly Mia Stewart

Created by
FRANCINE PASCAL

Illustrated by
Ying-Hwa Hu

A BANTAM SKYLARK BOOK ®
NEW YORK · TORONTO · LONDON · SYDNEY · AUCKLAND

To Lisa Yacov

RL 2, ages 005–008

A Bantam Skylark Book / September 1990

Sweet Valley High® und Sweet Valley Kids are trademarks of Francine Pascal

Conceived by Francine Pascal

*Produced by Daniel Weiss Associates, Inc.
33 West 17th Street
New York, NY 10011*

Cover art by Susan Tang

Skylark Books is a registered trademark of Bantam Books, a division of Bantam Doubleday Dell Publishing Group, Inc.

ISBN 0-553-15818-X

Published simultaneously in the United States and Canada

Bantam Books are published by Bantam Books, a division of Bantam Doubleday Dell Publishing Group, Inc. Its trademark, consisting of the words "Bantam Books" and the portrayal of a rooster, is Registered in U.S. Patent and Trademark Office and in other countries. Marca Registrada. Bantam Books, 666 Fifth Avenue, New York, New York 10103.

PRINTED IN THE UNITED STATES OF AMERICA

OPM   0 9 8 7 6 5 4 3 2 1

CHAPTER 1

Two-Wheelers

"Last one to the park is a rotten string bean!" Jessica Wakefield called to her twin sister, Elizabeth. Jessica jumped onto her bicycle and pedaled out of the Wakefields' driveway.

Elizabeth swung her leg over her bicycle seat and followed close behind. "No fair!" she yelled. "You got a head start."

The two girls raced toward Charles Fremont Park. Soon Elizabeth passed Jessica. As they got closer to the park, both girls were even. "It's a tie," Elizabeth said, out of breath.

Jessica and Elizabeth loved to race to the park and they almost always got there at the same time. They loved doing many things together. They shared a bedroom, they shared pencils and toys, and they always split candy bars in half. Jessica and Elizabeth were identical twins. They were also best friends.

The two girls looked exactly alike. They both had blue-green eyes and long blond hair with bangs. When they dressed alike, even their friends in second grade couldn't tell them apart.

It was easy to tell which twin was which when they were in the park. Elizabeth always rushed to the jungle gym first, while Jessica preferred to skip rope. Or Elizabeth would play pirates and space explorers with some of the boys while Jessica would play hopscotch with some of the girls. Even though they looked alike they didn't always like the same things.

"Jessica." Lila Fowler rode over on her shiny blue bike to say hello. "Do you want to try double-Dutch jump rope?" she asked.

"Sure," Jessica said. She looked at her sister to see if Elizabeth wanted to join them.

"No, thanks," Elizabeth said. She didn't like Lila very much and wanted to play with her own friends. While Jessica and Lila rode away, she looked around the playground. She saw Amy Sutton and Eva Simpson taking turns going down the slide.

"Wooo-ooo-ooo-oo!" Amy shouted as she went down. "Hi, Elizabeth."

Elizabeth wheeled her bike over to the trees. She was about to put down the kickstand when Todd Wilkins rode up next to her. "Do you want to have a bike race?" he asked.

"Sure," Elizabeth said. "But I'm so fast I might beat you," she added with a grin.

"You wish!" Todd said. He and Elizabeth loved to tease each other.

"Are you going to race?" Eva called, as she slid down the slide. "Hurry, Amy! Elizabeth and Todd are going to have a bike race."

"Great," Amy called from the top of the slide. "I know Elizabeth will win."

Ken Matthews, one of Todd's friends, pointed at Elizabeth's bicycle. "You can't race against a girl's bike," he said, laughing.

4

"I guess it wouldn't be fair," Todd said. "I'd win by too much," he added with a smile.

"At least Elizabeth doesn't need training wheels anymore," Winston Egbert teased. He looked over at the entrance to the park. "Like some people."

Elizabeth saw Lois Waller riding into the park. Her mother was walking beside her. Lois was the only one in their class who still had training wheels on her bicycle. She was always being teased because she was so chubby, and she cried at almost anything. Mrs. Waller kissed Lois on the cheek and then went to talk to some of the other mothers.

"What a baby," Ken said. He and Todd began to laugh.

"She is not," Elizabeth said, sticking up

6

for Lois. "Maybe she's almost ready to ride a two-wheeler."

Jessica and Lila ran over to join the group. "What are you talking about?" Lila wanted to know.

"Crybaby's here," Ken laughed.

"Oh, look out. Here she comes," Todd whispered.

Elizabeth gave him an angry look. "Don't be mean," she said. She smiled at Lois as she rode over. "Hi."

"Hi, Elizabeth," Lois said shyly.

"When are you going to ride a real bike?" Lila asked.

"That's right," Jessica chimed in. "Maybe you should still be riding a tricycle."

Everyone but Elizabeth laughed. Lois looked sad. "My mother doesn't want me to get hurt," she explained.

7

Elizabeth wheeled her bike forward a few inches. "Do you want to try mine?" she asked. "I'll help you. It's really easy."

"No," Lois whispered.

"Come on, everyone," Lila said loudly. "Let's go play."

"OK," Ken said. "Let's play Robin Hood."

Everyone ran to the other end of the park. Only Elizabeth stayed behind with Lois. "Do you want to play with us?" she asked.

Lois shook her head again and looked down at the ground. "No. I don't know how to play Robin Hood."

"There's no real way to play," Elizabeth explained. "You just make it up as you go along. It's really easy."

Lois's cheeks turned pink. "No, thanks."

Elizabeth wished Lois weren't so afraid

to try new things. She knew she'd have fun if she played with everyone else. Elizabeth liked Lois. Lois was nice and easy to get along with, but she was very shy. When their teacher, Ms. Becker, got married and became Mrs. Otis, it was Lois who picked out the perfect present. Elizabeth wished she could make Lois see how helpful she was.

"I have to go," Elizabeth said. "But if you want to play Robin Hood, just come right over."

"OK. Bye, Elizabeth." Lois sniffed.

Elizabeth ran to join her friends. She hoped she could figure out a way to help Lois stop being scared of everything.

CHAPTER 2

The Perfect Snack

Jessica zigzagged her bike across the sidewalk. "I hope Mom has a good snack waiting for us."

"Me, too," Elizabeth said.

The girls turned the corner onto their own street. Jessica stopped her bike in front of the Brants' house. Mr. and Mrs. Brant had just moved into the neighborhood. "I wonder if they have kids our age," Jessica said.

"Mom and Dad said they don't," Elizabeth answered.

"Look!" Jessica pointed to a large tree in the Brants' front yard. "Apples!"

Elizabeth stood up on her pedals to look. "Wow! Every branch has shiny red apples on it."

"I wonder if we could reach one," Jessica said. She lay her bicycle down on the grass and started to walk on the lawn, but Elizabeth grabbed her arm. "Jess. You can't just go into someone's yard. We haven't even met Mr. and Mrs. Brant yet."

Jessica frowned. There were many orange and apricot and lemon trees in their neighborhood, but no one else had an apple tree. She glanced at the apples again. They looked delicious. "We could just get one," she whispered to her sister.

Elizabeth shook her head. "We can't."

"Oh, OK," Jessica said. But she decided

12

not to give up. She thought it would be simple to sneak into the yard and grab an apple or two. They could easily run away before anyone saw them.

"And, Jess," Elizabeth said. "We have apples at home. Mom buys them all the time."

Jessica nodded. She got on her bike again. She wanted to come up with a plan to get some apples, but she would have to do some thinking first. "Lila says she's going to get a pony for her birthday," she said, changing the subject. Lila's parents were very rich, and she always got great presents. Sometimes Jessica felt a little jealous of Lila.

"A pony," Elizabeth said. "What a wonderful present. Remember the pony ride we had at Wild West Town?" She and

Jessica and Steven had been there with Grandma and Grandpa Wakefield.

Jessica nodded. "I'll bet I could ride a bucking bronco if I tried," she boasted.

Elizabeth laughed. "I think you'd be scared."

"I would not." Jessica shook her head. "I'm not a baby like Lois Waller."

"She's not a baby," Elizabeth said.

Jessica made a face. "She's a crybaby, and you know it. No one else is such a scaredy-cat. She's the last one to have training wheels on her bike."

"She'll learn when she's ready," Elizabeth said quietly.

"When she's a million years old." Jessica giggled. She looked over at her sister. Elizabeth was always nice to everyone. Why did Elizabeth have to be so nice to crybaby Lois?

15

CHAPTER 3

A Practical Joke

It was Monday morning. Elizabeth had already changed into her paint smock and walked over to feed the class hamsters. "Hi, Tinkerbell. Hi, Thumbelina," she said. The hamsters looked out at her and wiggled their noses.

"Hi, Elizabeth," said a soft voice behind her. Elizabeth turned around. Lois Waller was holding a small bag of peanuts.

"Hi, Lois. Are those for the hamsters?" Elizabeth asked.

Lois nodded. "I wish I could have

hamsters at home. They're so cute. We have three cats, though, so my mom says I can't," she explained.

Lois fit two peanuts through the cage bars. The hamsters picked them up in their small paws and began to chew on the shells.

Elizabeth smiled. "That was nice of you to give them some peanuts," she said. "But I think we have to take them out of their shells."

Lois's cheeks turned pink. She and Elizabeth took five peanuts out of their shells and fed them to the hamsters. When they were done, Lois put down the bag of peanuts and tugged on her large purple sweater. Lois wore the sweater as often as she could, because she thought it made her look less chubby.

"I have to take my sweater off, because I'll be too hot under my smock," Lois said. "I hope no one teases me, though."

"They won't," Elizabeth told her. "Let's get our seats at the art table."

Everyone dipped their thick brushes into the jars of paint and had fun drawing outer-space creatures. When they were cleaning up, Lois gasped. "Where's my sweater?"

Charlie Cashman and Jerry McAllister began to snicker. "Where's my sweater? Boo hoo!" Charlie imitated Lois's voice.

"Mrs. Otis," Caroline Pearce called out to their teacher. "Somebody has Lois's sweater!"

Lois began to cry. "It's my favorite sweater. I just took it off to put my smock on."

"We'll find it," Mrs. Otis reassured her. She pointed to Charlie. "Do you know where the sweater is?"

Charlie shrugged his shoulders. He walked over to the windowsill and looked in a box of art supplies. "Oh, here it is," he said, pretending to be surprised.

Some of the boys began to laugh, and that made Lois cry harder. Mrs. Otis helped her put the sweater on again and patted her on the shoulder, but that didn't make Lois stop crying.

"Don't feel bad," Elizabeth said. "At least you got your sweater back."

"Why are they always so mean to me?" Lois wiped the tears off her cheeks.

"They tease you," Elizabeth said, "because they know you'll cry."

Lois sniffled. "I can't help it."

20

"Lois," Lila said as she walked over. "Charlie and Jerry are horrible, aren't they?"

Lois nodded, but she looked surprised that Lila was talking to her. Jessica came over, too. "We hate those boys," she said. "They are so dumb."

Elizabeth wondered why Jessica and Lila were suddenly being so nice to Lois. Were they about to tease her, too?

"Did you bring your new jump rope to school?" Lila asked Lois. "It's a really nice one."

"Do you want to use it?" Lois said with a smile. She looked very happy. "You can use it with me during recess."

"Great!" Jessica said.

Elizabeth was glad her sister was being nice to Lois. She knew everyone would like Lois if they only gave her a chance.

During recess, Lila and Jessica and Ellen Riteman took Lois's jump rope and then wouldn't let her play with them.

"We already have enough people," Lila told Lois. "Two to hold the rope and one to jump."

Lois tugged her sweater down and went off to sit on a bench.

Elizabeth had been watching the other girls. Now she walked over and stood with her hands on her hips. "That's Lois's jump rope," she said angrily. "You can't keep her from playing."

"Oh, all right. She can have her turn," Jessica said. "But tell her to hurry up."

Lois ran over quickly. She looked so happy to be included at last that she forgot how mean everyone was being.

"You should have *made* them let you

play," Elizabeth told her as they were walking back to their classroom. But she knew Lois was too shy to stand up for herself.

CHAPTER 4

Practice Makes Perfect

After school, Elizabeth and Jessica ate a snack at home and then rode their bikes to the park. Elizabeth rushed over to the monkey bars. She had climbed to the top when she heard someone laughing. "Go away, crybaby. You're probably afraid of heights, anyway," she heard a voice say.

Elizabeth looked down through the bars. Lois was standing on the ground. Ken Matthews was laughing at her. "I want to talk to Elizabeth," Lois said. Her voice was shaking.

"Try climbing up," Elizabeth called. "It's not that high."

Lois shook her head. "Can't you come down?"

"Sure," Elizabeth said, climbing down low enough until she could jump. She landed in the sand. "That was fun."

"I wish I could do that," Lois said. "But I'm afraid I'll fall."

Elizabeth sat on the lowest bar. "Just try climbing this far."

Lois shook her head again.

"How about going on the swings?" Elizabeth asked.

"OK. But I'm not supposed to swing very high," Lois said.

Elizabeth and Lois waited for turns on the swings. When Elizabeth got on, she pumped so hard she felt like she was flying. Lois just swung back and forth close to the ground.

"Don't be afraid, Lois. You won't fall," Elizabeth said. "Do you want me to push you?"

"No!" Lois said quickly. "I get dizzy when I swing too high."

Elizabeth sighed. She wished something she said would help Lois. "Just try—"

"I can't," Lois repeated. "That's why no one likes me."

"I like you," Elizabeth said.

Lois looked at her. "Really?"

Elizabeth smiled. "Sure. I have an idea." She got off the swing and ran over to her bicycle. Lois followed her. "I'll help you ride my bike, so the other kids won't make fun of you," she said.

"I can't—" Lois began.

"Yes, you can. I'll help," Elizabeth said firmly. She walked her bike to a quiet corner of the playground. "Please try, Lois," she said.

Lois looked worried. She glanced over her shoulder and then looked at the bike. "Promise you won't let go?"

"I promise," Elizabeth said.

"OK," Lois said, but she didn't sound so sure. She got on the seat while Elizabeth held the bike steady.

"Now put your feet on the pedals," Elizabeth said. She was trying to remember how her father had taught her. She and Jessica had learned to ride two-wheelers when they were six. They hadn't found it hard to give up their training wheels. "Keep the handlebar straight and then start to pedal," Elizabeth added.

Lois's hands were shaking, but she managed to pedal a short distance. The bike began tilting and Elizabeth couldn't get it steady again. Lois fell over onto the dirt.

"Are you OK?" Elizabeth asked.

Lois looked at her hands. They were scraped and dirty. Her chin was trembling, and two tears rolled down her cheeks. "Yes," she whispered.

"Just try once more," Elizabeth said. "This time I'll hold it even steadier. OK?"

"All right." Lois was trying hard not to cry. She climbed on the bicycle seat, and Elizabeth helped her to push off. Lois rode a little bit farther before she fell again.

"I'm sorry," Elizabeth said as she helped Lois stand up. "I know you'll get it this time."

Lois nodded quickly, and wiped a tear off

her cheek. "I don't want anyone to tease me anymore," she said.

On her third try, Lois went as far as the entrance to the park before she started wobbling. Elizabeth grabbed her quickly. "That was great," she said.

Lois smiled. "I went far, didn't I?" she asked.

"Yes," Elizabeth said happily. "Let's keep practicing. I'll bet by the time we go home, you'll be ready to ride on your own."

"I sure hope so," Lois said. "Maybe I'm not such a scaredy-cat after all."

CHAPTER 5

Lila's Plan

The next day Jessica stood in the lunch line with Lila. "What do you have for lunch?" she asked.

- "I brought a turkey sandwich that comes from a special store," Lila answered. "With three double-chocolate-chip cookies and a bag of pretzel sticks."

Jessica frowned. Lila's lunch always seemed much better than hers did. "I only have a peanut butter and jelly sandwich. I'll give you half of mine for half of yours."

Lila took a few seconds to answer. "OK,"

she finally said. "Why was Elizabeth playing with Lois yesterday at the park? Does she like Lois?"

Jessica shook her head. "Oh, no. She just feels sorry for Lois." But Jessica wasn't so sure. She didn't want her sister to be friends with the class crybaby.

"*You* don't like her, do you?" Lila went on.

"Of course not," Jessica said. "She's too much of a baby for me."

Lila looked over her shoulder to make sure no one was listening. "Do you want to play a joke on Lois?" she whispered.

"No!" Jessica gasped. She loved to play jokes. But she knew it would be mean to play a joke on Lois. "What do you want to do?" she asked.

"I have a bunch of ponytail holders," Lila

whispered. "Let's put our hair in the same pigtails as Lois and then let's start to cry. Won't that be funny? Ellen can do it, too."

Jessica took a milk carton from the refrigerator compartment. Elizabeth would probably be angry. She could always say it was Lila's idea.

At recess, Jessica, Ellen, and Lila put their hair up in pigtails. "Let's wait until everyone sees us," Lila ordered.

A few kids were looking at Todd's dinosaur book. Lois was standing nearby. She looked like she wanted to be part of the group.

Jessica, Lila, and Ellen walked over to Todd. "Can we look?" Ellen sniffled. She puffed her cheeks out to look chubby. "We want to look but we're scared!"

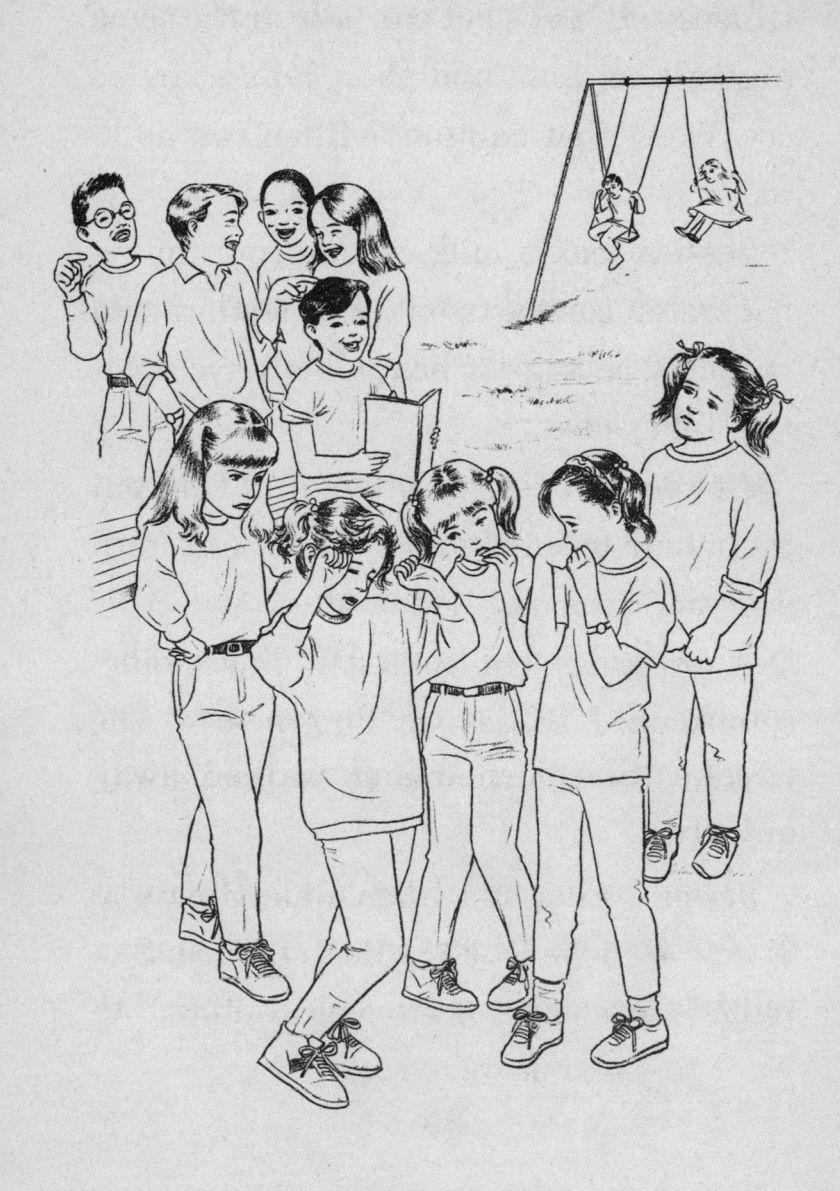

"Don't make fun of me," Lila said, trying to sound like Lois.

Jessica stuck her bottom lip out and squeezed her eyes shut. "Boo hoo," she wailed.

The other kids stared at them, then Winston Egbert started to laugh. "They're Lois!" he yelled.

Jessica and Ellen pretended to cry even harder. "Waaa!" they sobbed.

Everyone began to laugh at the girls' joke. Only Lois was quiet. Her face was becoming very red, and tears ran down her cheeks. She turned and walked away quickly.

"That wasn't funny at all," Elizabeth said to Jessica. "It was mean. I'm going to tell her you didn't mean it. And then I'm inviting her over to play at our house tomorrow afternoon."

"What?" Jessica's mouth dropped open. "You can't do that."

"I can do it. Just you watch," Elizabeth said. She began to walk away.

"Lila is coming over tomorrow," Jessica said.

Elizabeth ignored her.

"You can't invite crybaby over to our house," Jessica called. She crossed her arms and frowned.

"I can," said Elizabeth, and she headed across the playground. Lois was standing by the school building. Elizabeth put her arm around Lois's shoulder.

Jessica watched her sister.

"It was just a joke," she said, kicking a pebble. "It's all Lois's fault for crying."

Lila nodded. "She'll never change."

Jessica kicked the pebble again. She knew Elizabeth was angry with her, and Jessica knew just who to blame: Lois.

CHAPTER 6

After-School Plans

Lois wore her purple sweater to school on Wednesday. "I can't wait to go to your house today," she told Elizabeth before class began. "We'll have so much fun."

Elizabeth smiled. She was glad Lois was happy about coming over to play. "Lila will be there, too," she said. "I hope you don't mind."

"No," Lois said. She looked over at Lila and Jessica. "Maybe we can all play together."

"Maybe," Elizabeth said. She hoped Lila wouldn't be mean.

When Elizabeth and Lois got on the school bus at the end of the day, Jessica and Lila were already sitting together. Elizabeth and Lois sat down in front of them.

"Hi, Jessica. Hi, Lila," Lois said with a friendly smile.

Jessica frowned at Lila. "Did you hear a noise?"

"No," Lila said, shaking her head.

"I said hi," Lois repeated. "We're going to have so much fun, aren't we?"

"What did you say, Jessica?" Lila asked.

Elizabeth turned around and stared at her sister and Lila. "Quit it," she warned. "They're just acting dumb," she told Lois. "Don't pay any attention to them."

"Why aren't they listening to me?" Lois wanted to know.

No one answered her.

"What should we do first when we get home?" Jessica asked.

Lois felt better. She thought Jessica was finally including her in the conversation. "We could play dolls, or—"

"Let's play shopping trip," Lila interrupted. "We can each list what we'd buy if we had all the money in the world."

"That sounds like fun," Lois said. "If I could get anything, I would—"

"Let's pretend we take gymnastics class," Jessica cut in. She looked at Lila and Elizabeth. "We can pretend our stone wall is a balance beam."

"What if I fall off?" Lois asked.

Elizabeth gave her a friendly smile. "We

41

don't have to do what they do," she said. "We can play a different game."

"I want to do the balance beam," Lois said bravely. "I could try."

Lila and Jessica started giggling. "You could *try!*" Lila repeated, imitating Lois.

"You'd just fall off, Lois," Jessica said. "We can't let you play gymnastics class with us. You'd only cry. And that wouldn't be fun for us."

"Jessica!" Elizabeth said. She felt terrible that her own sister could act so mean.

Lois sniffled a little bit, but she kept her chin up. "I wouldn't cry," she said, tugging on her sweater. "I promise."

"Well, we're not taking any chances," Lila said.

Elizabeth felt angry at her sister. She folded her arms and tried to think of some-

thing that would cheer up Lois. "If you want," she said, "I can hold your hand while you go along the balance beam. That way you won't fall."

"Would you?" Lois asked. She smiled hopefully at Elizabeth. "I know I could do it if you helped me."

"On second thought, Jessica," Lila said from the seat behind them, "let's not play gymnastics class."

"Fine with me," Jessica said.

Lois looked like she was going to cry.

Elizabeth felt terrible. How would they ever get through the afternoon if Jessica and Lila were going to be so mean?

CHAPTER 7

I Dare You

When the bus came to their stop, Jessica, Lila, Elizabeth, and Lois got off. Jessica and Elizabeth's brother, Steven, and Todd Wilkins jumped off behind them.

"Come on, Lila," Jessica said. "Let's hurry to my house."

"Hey, Lois," Todd called. "Where are your training wheels?"

"Cut it out, Todd," Elizabeth told him. "If you don't, I won't ever play softball with you again."

Jessica and Lila laughed.

"You still have training wheels?" Steven asked Lois. He was in fourth grade, and he pretended he was a grown-up sometimes.

When Lois didn't say anything, Steven screamed. "Aaaah," he gasped, holding his neck. "I'm stuck in a nursery school."

Jessica laughed. "No, it's Lois who's the baby, Steven," she said. "And you'd better be nice to her or she'll start to cry."

"Don't listen to them, Lois," Elizabeth said. "Who wants to play with them anyway?" She glared at Jessica and stuck out her tongue.

Jessica didn't understand why her sister kept sticking up for Lois. She had to find a way to show Elizabeth that Lois would always be a crybaby. She jumped over a crack on the sidewalk and thought about the apple tree in the Brants' yard. She ran ahead until she was in front of the Brants' driveway. The apples looked even redder than before. They looked shiny and delicious.

"Lois," Jessica said slowly. She turned around as the others caught up to her. "You can play with us and we'll be nice to you."

"OK," Lois said in a happy voice.

Lila looked surprised. Jessica whispered in her ear. "I'm going to tell Lois to climb that apple tree and to pick some apples for us. But I'll bet she's too afraid to do it."

A big smile spread across Lila's face. "That's right, Lois," she said. "You can play dolls and shopping trip with us if you do one little thing."

"What?" Lois asked. She looked nervously at Elizabeth.

47

"See that tree over there?" Jessica said, pointing to the apple tree.

Lois nodded.

"If you climb it and get some apples for all of us, you can—"

"No way!" Elizabeth interrupted. She shook her head and walked over to Jessica. "You know we aren't supposed to climb trees in other peoples' yards. And those aren't our apples, so we can't take any."

Jessica shrugged her shoulders. "It doesn't matter. Lois wouldn't do it anyway."

"That's right," Lila added. "Lois is too much of a fraidy-cat to do an easy thing like that."

Todd looked surprised. "You couldn't climb a little tree like that?" he asked Lois. "It's so easy. I could probably go all the way to the top in ten seconds."

"So could I," Steven boasted. "That's the simplest kind of tree to climb. Look how the branches go out sideways."

Lois was staring at the apple tree and pulling nervously at her sweater. "I've never climbed a tree before," she said softly.

"See?" Todd laughed. "She won't do it."

Jessica smiled. "If you don't want to do it, you don't have to, Lois. But Lila and I are going home to play without you, now."

"No!" Lois spoke up.

"Look out. She's going to cry," Steven teased.

"You be quiet," Elizabeth told him angrily. "You don't have to do anything you don't want to, Lois," she went on. "Don't listen to them."

"I'll do it," Lois whispered.

49

"All right!" Todd shouted. Jessica and Lila looked at each other and smiled. This was going to be fun.

Elizabeth grabbed Lois's hand. "Lois, don't. We don't have permission to climb that tree."

"If she wants to do it, let her," Lila said. She pointed to the apple tree. "Go ahead, Lois. We're waiting."

CHAPTER 8

Lois to the Rescue

Elizabeth watched as the others tiptoed into the Brants' yard. She bit her lip.

Lois was leading the way. "I guess you are brave," Lila said from behind. Elizabeth knew Lila didn't mean it. She also knew that if Lois did not climb the tree, the others would tease her even more than before.

Elizabeth followed them to try one last time to stop them. "Let's get out of here," she warned, looking at the house. "We shouldn't be here."

"Don't be a spoilsport," Steven said.

Lois was staring with round eyes up at the tree. Then she looked down at the rotten apples on the ground.

"Do it, Lois," Jessica said. "It'll be easy." Jessica and Lila were grinning.

Elizabeth stood next to Lois. "Don't let them bully you."

"I won't," Lois said stubbornly. "I'm not a scaredy-cat anymore. I can climb any tree."

Elizabeth's stomach flip-flopped. She could tell Lois didn't really feel very brave. "Have you really never climbed a tree before?" she asked.

Lois nodded. Todd and Steven laughed.

"It's about time you learned," Lila said.

"Be quiet," Elizabeth said. She looked at Lois. "You don't have to do it, you know."

"Yes, I do," Lois said. She grabbed the lowest branch.

"Go ahead. We'll give you a push," Jessica suggested. She was grinning from ear to ear.

Elizabeth had done all she could to help Lois. Now she crossed her fingers, while Jessica and Steven helped Lois up.

"Just climb it like a ladder," Todd called up.

Lois was standing on the lowest branch. Her eyes were squeezed shut.

"Go on, Lois. You said you weren't scared anymore," Lila teased.

Lois gulped and reached for another branch. Elizabeth held her breath. "Be careful," she said.

All five of them watched Lois put one foot on the branch. A piece of bark fell to the ground.

"Go on, Lois," Jessica said. "The good apples are a little higher."

Lois nodded without saying anything. She didn't move.

"Keep going," Lila yelled. She nudged Jessica in the ribs and they giggled.

Elizabeth glared at them. "You can stop if you don't want to go any higher," she called up to Lois. "You already showed us you aren't scared."

"But she didn't get any apples, Liz," Jessica reminded her. "It doesn't count until she picks some apples."

Elizabeth kicked a rotten apple toward her sister. "Eat this one," she grumbled.

"She's not moving," Steven whispered. "She's too scared to move."

Then Elizabeth heard a "meow." "What was that?" she asked.

Lois slowly opened her eyes and looked above her. "There's a kitten up here," she said calmly. "I think it's afraid to come down."

"I'll get it," Steven said, pushing in front of the others. But Lois was already starting to climb higher. She grabbed onto the branches to pull herself up. "Here, kitty, kitty," she repeated gently. The kitten meowed again.

Jessica's mouth dropped open. "Lois is rescuing the kitten," she said in surprise.

Just then, the door of the Brants' house opened.

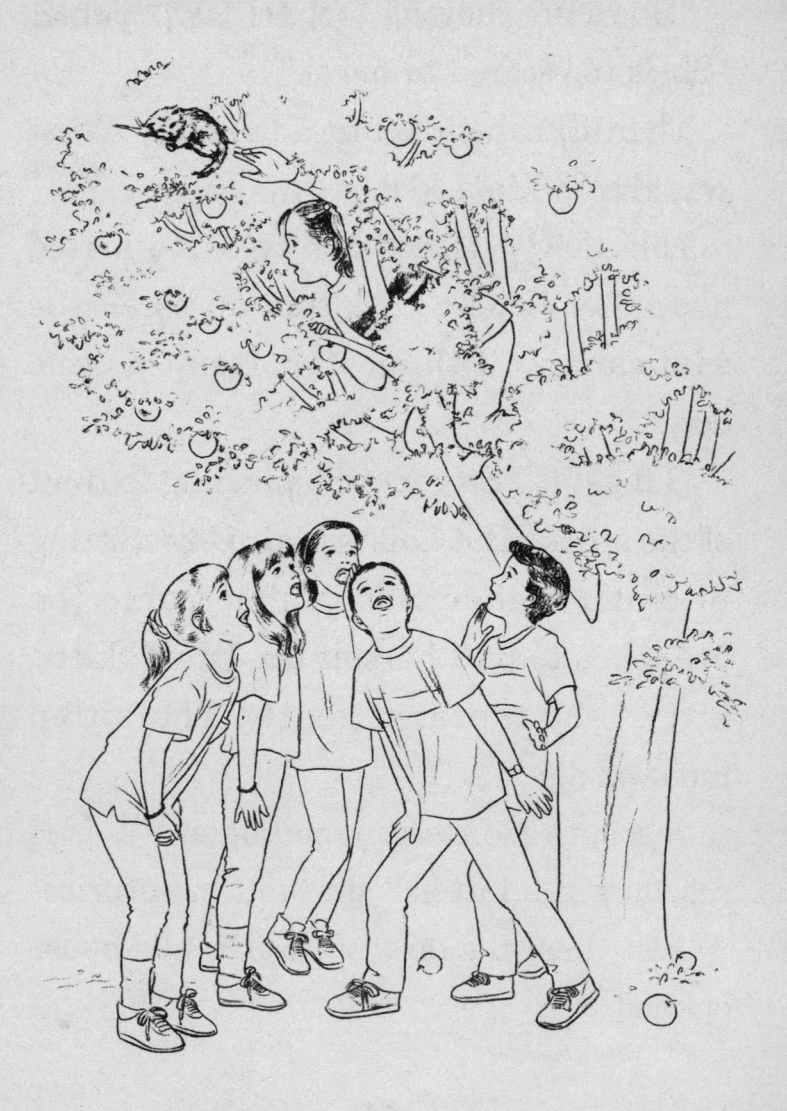

"WHAT'S GOING ON HERE?" yelled Mrs. Brant.

Elizabeth jumped in surprise. Then Jessica grabbed her hand, and they started to run.

CHAPTER 9

Lois Saves the Day

"You come back here, kids!" Mrs. Brant shouted.

Jessica wanted to run all the way home, but Elizabeth tugged on her arm. "We have to go back," she said.

Lila, Todd, Elizabeth, Jessica, and Steven walked back into the yard. Mrs. Brant walked out of the house to talk to them. She was wearing tan pants, a sweatshirt, and sneakers. She looked like she could be nice, but right now she looked angry.

"You kids wait here," she said, before

walking up to the tree. "Come down from there right now," she shouted to Lois.

Jessica expected to hear Lois start to cry, but Lois didn't. "I'm trying to reach a kitten," she called from the leafy branches. "It's scared and won't come down."

Elizabeth ran over to Mrs. Brant. "We didn't mean to come into your yard," she began. "We wanted some apples, and then—"

"Is that Bitsy?" Mrs. Brant said to Lois. "That's very sweet of you to rescue her, but you should have come and told me. It's dangerous to climb trees by yourself."

Jessica stared at Lila. The kitten belonged to Mrs. Brant. Lois was getting all the credit for climbing the tree and rescuing it!

"Now just wait here," Mrs. Brant said.

She went to the garage and came back carrying a stepladder.

"Can you reach Bitsy?" she asked as she put the ladder beside the tree.

"I have her," Lois called down. "She's really scared. I have to calm her down."

Mrs. Brant climbed up the ladder. "Hand her to me, and then climb down the ladder," she told Lois. When Mrs. Brant came down, she held a tiny, trembling, black kitten in her arms.

"Oh," Elizabeth said, patting the kitten's head. "It's so cute."

Jessica felt terrible. She and Lila were silent as Lois climbed down the ladder.

"I rescued her," Lois said happily as she jumped down from the last step. "I felt so sorry for her because I knew how scared she was."

"You climbed really high," Todd said. He sounded impressed.

Elizabeth was smiling. "See, you *are* brave," she told Lois. Lois's cheeks turned bright pink, and she shook her head shyly.

"Yes, you are," Mrs. Brant agreed. "Still, you shouldn't have climbed the tree without asking permission first."

"We're sorry," Elizabeth said quickly.

"Apology accepted," Mrs. Brant said with a smile. "Now how about a reward of apples?"

"Hooray!" Steven yelled. "Apples from a real apple tree."

"But this time, I'll do the climbing," Mrs. Brant said, smiling.

Jessica was so surprised by how things had turned out that she didn't know what to say. Mrs. Brant handed Bitsy to Lois, and then climbed back up the ladder. "Catch," she said. She tossed an apple down to Todd. "Catch," she repeated, tossing one to Steven.

"This is fun." Elizabeth laughed as she caught one, too.

Soon, a big pile of red, ripe apples was on the grass.

Everyone ate their apples happily. Jessica sat next to Lois so she could pat the kitten. Bitsy purred loudly.

"I can tell she likes you," Jessica told Lois quietly. "She's very pretty. I'm glad you rescued her."

Lois smiled at Jessica. "Me, too."

"We sure have a lot of apples," Lila said. "What are we going to do with them?" She sat on the other side of Lois to pat Bitsy, too.

"Hey, I know," Lois said. She looked at Jessica. "Only if you want to," she went on.

Jessica smiled. "What? Tell us."

"We could make applesauce."

"That's a great idea," Elizabeth said. "Lois, you're the star of the day!"

CHAPTER 10

Bobbing for Apples

Mrs. Brant gave the kids a shopping bag and Elizabeth and Lois filled the bag with the apples. Then they carried the heavy bag between them back to the Wakefield house to make applesauce.

"Well, hello." Mrs. Wakefield greeted them as they walked through the kitchen door. "I was beginning to wonder where you were."

"We got apples from Mrs. Brant down the street," Elizabeth explained. "She's nice. And Lois rescued her kitten."

"Lois was brave," Jessica said. She poked Lila's arm, and Lila nodded.

"Rescuing kittens is a very special thing to do," Mrs. Wakefield said with a big smile for Lois. "I'm very proud of you."

Lois had a wide grin on her face. "I thought I would be scared but I wasn't, was I, Elizabeth?"

"No." Elizabeth grinned back.

"And we want to make applesauce," Jessica said. "Can we, Mom?"

Mrs. Wakefield snapped her fingers. "That's a wonderful idea. Was it yours, Lois?"

Lois nodded and turned pink. But she didn't turn pink because she was scared or about to cry. This time she turned pink because she was happy. "Yes, it was my idea," she whispered shyly.

"One batch of applesauce coming up," Mrs. Wakefield announced. "First we'll need to wash the apples."

"There're too many to fit in the sink, Mom," Steven said, looking in the bag.

"We can use the big washbasin outside," Elizabeth suggested.

"Let's give those apples a bath," Jessica said. She and Lila carried the shopping bag full of apples outside. Then they filled the basin with water and put the apples in the basin. The apples began to float in the water.

"You know what this reminds me of?" Jessica said.

Elizabeth nodded. "I know. Bobbing for apples."

"Let's try it," Lois giggled.

When the basin was full of apples and

water, the apples floated around and bumped into each other.

Todd pushed up his sleeves. "I'm an expert at this. Watch me." He leaned over the water and looked at the apples. Then he dunked his whole head in. Jessica screamed with laughter. When Todd took his head out of the water, his hair was plastered to his face. He looked funny but he had an apple between his teeth!

Elizabeth giggled. "Let me try." She wrinkled her nose and chose her apple. She tried to bite it with her teeth, but it bobbed away from her.

"It's like bumper cars in there," Lois said.

"Did you ever go on those?" Lila asked cheerfully.

Lois shook her head. "No, but I'm going

to, next time I'm at the amusement park. I'm not scared to try anymore."

"Hey, I thought we were washing these apples," Mrs. Wakefield said as she came outside.

"We are. And we're bobbing for them, too," Steven explained.

Elizabeth was still trying for her apple. She decided Todd's method was the best, so she took a deep breath and plunged her head in the water. She bit into the apple before it got away.

"You got it!" Jessica yelled when Elizabeth came up.

"I guess you kids are having an early Halloween this year," Mrs. Wakefield said with a laugh. "Does that mean you won't need to go trick-or-treating when the time comes?"

Elizabeth squeezed the water out of her ponytail and grinned. "No way, Mom. We're definitely dressing up and going trick-or-treating on Halloween."

Mrs. Wakefield smiled. "I thought so. You'd better start thinking about your costumes. Halloween is only two weeks away. And this year there's going to be a special surprise."

What's in store for Jessica and Elizabeth this year on Halloween? Find out in Sweet Valley Kids #12, **SWEET VALLEY TRICK OR TREAT.**

ENTER BANTAM BOOKS' SWEET VALLEY READER OF THE MONTH SWEEPSTAKES

OFFICIAL RULES:

READER OF THE MONTH ESSAY CONTEST

1. No Purchase Is Necessary. Enter by hand printing your name, address, date of birth and telephone number on a plain 3" x 5" card, and sending this card along with your essay telling us about yourself and why you like to read Sweet Valley books to:

READER OF THE MONTH
SWEET VALLEY KIDS
BANTAM BOOKS
YR MARKETING
666 FIFTH AVENUE
NEW YORK, NEW YORK 10103

2. Reader of the Month Contest Winner. For each month from June 1, 1990 through December 31, 1990, a Sweet Valley Kids Reader of the Month will be chosen from the entries received during that month. The winners will have their essay and photo published in the back of an upcoming Sweet Valley Kids title.

3. Enter as often as you wish, but each essay must be original and each entry must be mailed in a separate envelope bearing sufficient postage. All completed entries must be postmarked and received by Bantam no later than December 31, 1990, in order to be eligible for the Essay Contest and Sweepstakes. Entrants must be between the ages of 6 and 16 years old. Each essay must be no more than 150 words and must be typed double-spaced or neatly printed on one side of an 8 1/2" x 11" page which has the entrant's name, address, date of birth and telephone number at the top. The essays submitted will be judged each month by Bantam's Marketing Department on the basis of originality, creativity, thoughtfulness, and writing ability, and all of Bantam's decisions are final and binding. Essays become the property of Bantam Books and none will be returned. Bantam reserves the right to edit the winning essays for length and readability. Essay Contest winners will be notified by mail within 30 days of being chosen. In the event there are an insufficient number of essays received in any month which meet the minimum standards established by the judges, Bantam reserves the right not to choose a Reader of the Month. Winners have 30 days from the date of Bantam's notice in which to respond, or an alternate Reader of the Month winner will be chosen. Bantam is not responsible for incomplete or lost or misdirected entries.

4. Winners of the Essay Contest and their parents or legal guardians may be required to execute an Affidavit of Eligibility and Promotional Release supplied by Bantam. Entering the Reader of the Month Contest constitutes permission for use of the winner's name, address, likeness and contest submission for publicity and promotional purposes, with no additional compensation.

5. Employees of Bantam Books, Bantam Doubleday Dell Publishing Group, Inc., and their subsidiaries and affiliates, and their immediate family members are not eligible to enter the Essay Contest. The Essay Contest is open to residents of the U.S. and Canada (excluding the province of Quebec), and is void wherever prohibited or restricted by law. All applicable federal, state, and local regulations apply.

READER OF THE MONTH SWEEPSTAKES

6. Sweepstakes Entry. No purchase is necessary. Every entrant in the Sweet Valley High, Sweet Valley Twins and Sweet Valley Kids Essay Contest whose completed entry is received by December 31, 1990 will be entered in the Reader of the Month Sweepstakes. The Grand Prize winner will be selected in a random drawing from all completed entries received on or about February 1, 1991 and will be notified by mail. Bantam's decision is final and binding. Odds of winning are dependent on the number of entries received. The prize is non-transferable and no substitution is allowed. The Grand Prize winner must be accompanied on the trip by a parent or legal guardian. Taxes are the sole responsibility of the prize winner. Trip must be taken within one year of notification and is subject to availability. Travel arrangements will be made for the winner and, once made, no changes will be allowed.

7. 1 Grand Prize. A six day, five night trip for two to Los Angeles, California. Includes round-trip coach airfare, accommodations for 5 nights (economy double occupancy), a rental car -- economy model, and spending allowance for meals. (Approximate retail value: $4,500.)

8. The Grand Prize winner and their parent or legal guardian may be required to execute an Affidavit of Eligibility and Promotional Release supplied by Bantam. Entering the Reader of the Month Sweepstakes constitutes permission for use of the winner's name, address, and the likeness for publicity and promotional purposes, with no additional compensation.

9. Employees of Bantam Books, Bantam Doubleday Dell Publishing Group, Inc., and their subsidiaries and affiliates, and their immediate family members are not eligible to enter this Sweepstakes. The Sweepstakes is open to residents of the U.S. and Canada (excluding the province of Quebec), and is void wherever prohibited or restricted by law. If a Canadian resident, the Grand Prize winner will be required to correctly answer an arithmetical skill-testing question in order to receive the prize. All applicable federal, state, and local regulations apply. The Grand Prize will be awarded in the name of the minor's parent or guardian. Taxes, if any, are the winner's sole responsibility.

10. For the name of the Grand Prize winner and the names of the winners of the Sweet Valley High, Sweet Valley Twins and Sweet Valley Kids Essay Contests, send a stamped, self-addressed envelope entirely separate from your entry to: Bantam Books, Sweet Valley Reader of the Month Winners, Young Readers Marketing, 666 Fifth Avenue, New York, New York 10103. The winners list will be available after April 15, 1991.